CONTENTS

Young Cam Jansen
and the
Lions' Lunch Mystery

BY **DAVID A. ADLER**

ILLUSTRATED BY **SUSANNA NATTI**

PUFFIN BOOKS

For Michelle and Jonathan,
my Dutch cousins
—D.A.

To the Gosselins, John and Liz,
and to the gosling, Zack
—S.N.

PUFFIN BOOKS
Published by the Penguin Group
Penguin Young Readers Group, 345 Hudson Street, New York, New York 10014, U.S.A.
Penguin Group (Canada), 90 Eglinton Avenue East, Suite 700, Toronto, Ontario, Canada M4P 2Y3
(a division of Pearson Penguin Canada Inc.)
Penguin Books Ltd, 80 Strand, London WC2R 0RL, England
Penguin Ireland, 25 St Stephen's Green, Dublin 2, Ireland (a division of Penguin Books Ltd)
Penguin Group (Australia), 250 Camberwell Road, Camberwell, Victoria 3124, Australia
(a division of Pearson Australia Group Pty Ltd)
Penguin Books India Pvt Ltd, 11 Community Centre, Panchsheel Park, New Delhi - 110 017, India
Penguin Group (NZ), 67 Apollo Drive, Rosedale, North Shore 0632, New Zealand
(a division of Pearson New Zealand Ltd)
Penguin Books (South Africa) (Pty) Ltd, 24 Sturdee Avenue, Rosebank, Johannesburg 2196, South Africa

Registered Offices: Penguin Books Ltd, 80 Strand, London WC2R 0RL, England

First published in the United States of America by Viking, a division of Penguin Young Readers Group, 2007
Published by Puffin Books, a division of Penguin Young Readers Group, 2008

1 3 5 7 9 10 8 6 4 2

THE LIBRARY OF CONGRESS HAS CATALOGED THE VIKING EDITION AS FOLLOWS:
Adler, David A.
Young Cam Jansen and the lions' lunch mystery / by David A. Adler ; illustrated by Susanna Natti.
p. cm. – (Young Cam Jansen ; 13)
Summary: On a field trip to the zoo, Cam Jansen uses her photographic memory
to help solve what happened to Danny's lunch.
ISBN: 978-0-670-06171-6 (hardcover)
[1. Memory—Fiction. 2. School field trips—Fiction. 3. Zoos—Fiction. 4. Mystery and detective stories—Fiction.]
I. Natti, Susanna, ill. II. Title.
PZ7.A2615Yot 2007 [Fic]—dc22 2006029076

Puffin Books ISBN 978-0-14-241176-6
Puffin® and Easy-to-Read® are registered trademarks of Penguin Group (USA) Inc.

Printed in the United States of America
Set in Bookman

1. DANNY'S ZOO RIDDLE

"Is everyone here?" Ms. Dee asked.

The children in her class

were in the front of the room.

They were in line.

They were getting ready to visit the zoo.

A few parent helpers were there, too.

Danny got out of line.

"Please," he called out,

"help Ms. Dee. She wants to know

if we're all here, so if you're *not* here,

raise your hand."

Danny looked at Cam Jansen, Eric Shelton,

and the other children in Ms. Dee's class.

No one raised his hand.

"Great!" Danny said. "We're all here.

Now let's go to the zoo."

"That's not funny," Beth said.

"If someone is not here,

how can he raise his hand?"

"Get back in line," Ms. Dee told Danny.

Ms. Dee checked the list

of children in her class.

She looked to see if they were all in line.

Danny opened a small riddle book.

"Hey," he said. "Here's a zoo riddle.

What's gray and has sixteen wheels?"

Cam Jansen closed her eyes.

She said, *"Click!"*

Then she told Danny,

"An elephant on roller skates.

That riddle is on page thirty-six."

Cam smiled and said, "I read that book."

Cam has an amazing memory.

"My memory is like a camera," she says.

"I have pictures in my head

of everything I've seen."

She says *click!* is the sound

the camera in her head makes

when she wants to remember something.

Cam's real name is Jennifer.

But when people found out

about her amazing memory,

they called her "The Camera."

Soon "The Camera" became just "Cam."

"We're all here," Ms. Dee said.

"Now, please, follow me."

Cam opened her eyes.

She, the other children in her class,

and the parent helpers

followed Ms. Dee outside.

Other classes were already waiting.

Five buses were lined up

by the front curb of the school.

"Take your partner's hand,"

Ms. Dee said.

Cam took Eric's hand.

"Hey," Beth said.

"Where's *my* partner?

Where's Danny?"

2. LUNCH AT THE LIONS' DEN

Tweet! Tweet!

Ms. Dee blew her whistle.

"Danny, where are you?" she shouted.

Danny stuck his head through

an open window on the first bus.

"Here I am," he said.

"I'm ready to go to the zoo."

"Will you please

get off that bus," Ms. Dee told him.

"Wait here with the class."

Danny got off the bus.

Dr. Prell, the principal, came outside.

She spoke to the children.

"Stay with your group.

Listen to your teachers.

And have a great time at the zoo."

Dr. Prell walked back into the school.

"I hope everyone remembered to bring

a bag lunch and to write your name on it,"

Ms. Dee said.

"When you get on the bus,

drop the bag in the big box. It's in the front.

Then sit with your partner."

Ms. Dee led her class to the middle bus.

She stood by the door as the children got on.

The driver was Mrs. Lane.

A blue box and a yellow box

were in the front of Mrs. Lane's bus.

The blue box was marked "Lost and Found."

The yellow box was marked "Lunches."

Cam and Eric dropped their lunch bags

into the yellow box.

They found seats near the back of the bus.

Danny and Beth sat behind them.

After a short ride,

the bus stopped by thc front of the zoo.

As the children got off,

Ms. Dee told them to stay with their groups.

"We will meet for lunch at noon," she said.

"We will meet at the tables near the lions' den.

I'll bring the lunches."

Cam and Eric got off the bus.

They joined their group.

Mr. Kane, Beth's father, was their leader.

They went to the monkey house.

Danny pointed at a small monkey.

It was sitting on a swing.

The small monkey pointed at Danny.

Danny patted his head.

The monkey patted its head.

Danny waved to the monkey.

The monkey waved back.

Next they visited

the black bears and the seals.

Then Mr. Kane said,

"Let's go to the lions' den.

It's time for lunch."

Danny asked, "Is it time for the lions' lunch?"

"No," Mr. Kane answered.

"It's time for ours."

The yellow box from the bus

was on one of the tables

near the lions' den.

Ms. Dee took the lunches from the box

and gave them all out.

"Hey!" Danny shouted.

"Where's *my* lunch?"

3. LOST AND FOUND

"Is this a joke?" Ms. Dee asked Danny.

"No," he said. "I had a lunch.

I put it in the box."

"Maybe it fell out," Cam said.

"It's a long walk from the bus."

"May Cam and I go to the bus

to look for Danny's lunch?"

Eric asked Ms. Dee.

Ms. Dee looked at Mr. Kane.

"Beth and I will go with them," he said.

"I will, too," Danny said. "It's my lunch."

They walked through the zoo

to the parking lot.

"My lunch is in a brown bag,"

Danny said as they walked.

"My name is on it."

They walked slowly.

They looked for Danny's lunch.

But they didn't find it.

"There's the bus," Beth said.

Cam, Eric, Beth, and Danny ran to the bus.

"I lost my lunch," Danny told Mrs. Lane.

"I dropped it in the box and now it's gone."

Mrs. Lane put down the book she was reading.

It was a mystery.

"Maybe someone put on a disguise,"

Mrs. Lane said. "He dressed up as Danny

and took his lunch."

Mrs. Lane held up her book. "In this book

lots of people wear disguises."

Eric said, "I don't think someone

put on a Danny disguise.

I think Danny put his lunch

in the wrong box. I think

he dropped it in the blue box.

That's the Lost and Found box."

Eric looked through

the Lost and Found box.

He found pencils, mittens, and a baseball cap,

but he didn't find Danny's lunch.

4. CAM SAID, "CLICK!"

"You can have some of my lunch,"

Mrs. Lane said.

She gave Danny an apple

and a small bag of carrot sticks.

Mr. Kane said,

"And I'll buy you a sandwich and a drink.

Now let's go back to the lions' den."

Eric whispered to Cam,

"But we still don't know

what happened to Danny's lunch."

"Maybe Danny never brought his lunch,"

Cam said while they walked.

"Maybe he forgot it at home."

She told Eric to hold her hand.

"I don't want to bump into anyone."

Then Cam closed her eyes

and said, *"Click!"*

Cam said, "I'm looking at Danny

when we were in the front of our room.

He had his lunch.

It was in a brown bag."

Cam said, *"Click!"* again.

"Now I'm looking at Danny

when we were standing outside."

Cam said, *"Click!"* again.

"That's it!" she said.

She opened her eyes.

Mr. Kane was about to buy

a sandwich and juice for Danny.

"Wait!" Cam called, and ran to Mr. Kane.

"Don't buy Danny a sandwich.

I know where to find Danny's lunch."

5. A TREAT FOR EVERYONE

"Danny's lunch is with

one of the other classes," Cam said.

"It is?" Danny said.

"Yes," Cam told him.

"You were in a hurry this morning.

You were the first one on the bus."

"Ms. Dee told me to get off,

and I did," Danny said.

"I waited with the class."

Cam reminded Danny,

"When you got on alone,

you got on the first bus.

That's where you left your lunch.

Then our class got on the third bus."

Mr. Kane said, "Mr. Tan's class

is by the monkey house.

Danny's lunch must be with them."

Cam, Eric, Danny, Beth, and Mr. Kane

went to the tables where Mr. Tan's

class was sitting.

Danny's lunch was there in a green box.

Danny stopped by the monkey house.

He waved to the small monkey.

The small monkey jumped up and down
and waved back.

"He likes me," Danny said.

"Of course he does," Mr. Kane told Danny.

Cam, Eric, Danny, Beth, and Mr. Kane
returned to the lions' den.

Eric told Ms. Dee,

"Cam found Danny's lunch."

He told her how Cam solved the mystery.

"Great!" Ms. Dee said.

"Cam is lucky to have such a great memory,

and we're lucky she's in our class.

Now it's time for a treat.

I bought ice cream for everyone."

"Even for me?" Danny asked.

"Yes," Ms. Dee said, "even for you."

"Sometimes I'm silly," Danny said.

Ms. Dee agreed.

"But you're also lots of fun," she said.

"I'm glad you're in my class, too."

A Cam Jansen
Memory Game

Take another look at the picture on page 31.

Study it.

Blink your eyes and say, *"Click!"*

Then turn back to this page

and answer these questions:

1. Is Cam Jansen smiling?

2. Are there any birds in the picture?

3. What color are the tables?

4. Is there a banana on one of the tables?

5. How many children are sitting and eating
   ice cream?

6. How many lions are in the picture?